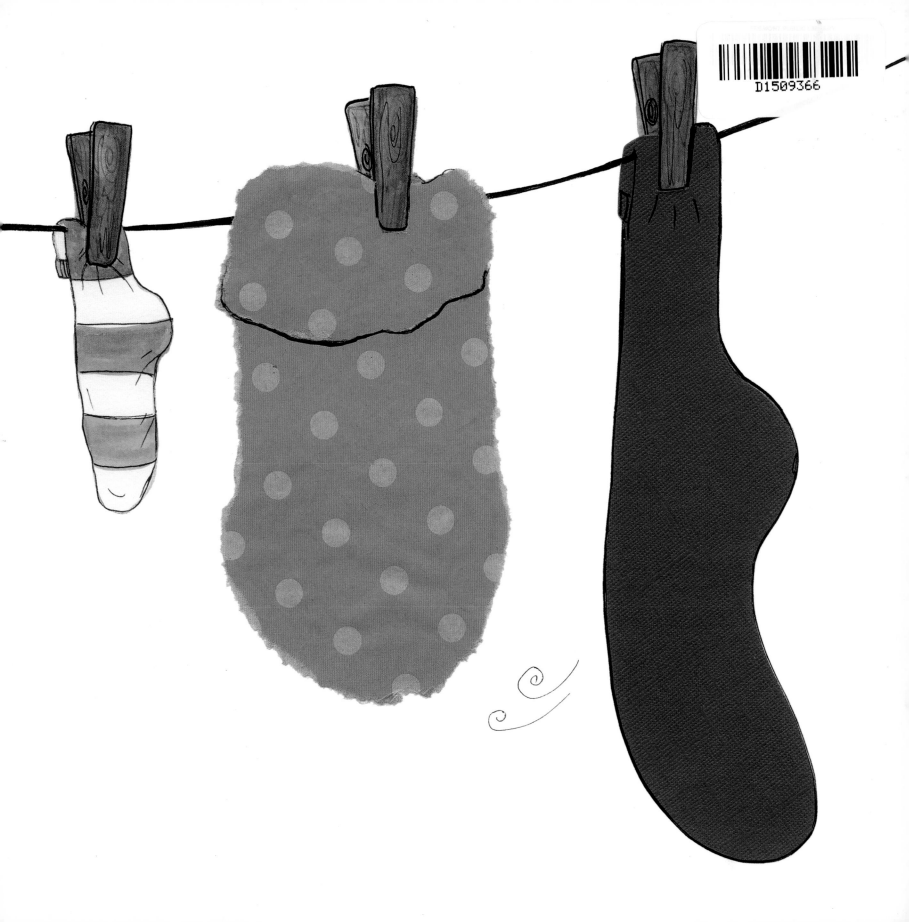

the Great Sock Secret

To Gwynne — Thank you for laughter, friendship and whimsical moments. I'm so glad I've shared the start of this adventure with you. – SW

For Bruce, who doesn't like odd socks. – GJ

First published 2016

EK Books
an imprint of Exisle Publishing Pty Ltd
'Moonrising', Narone Creek Road, Wollombi, NSW 2325, Australia
P.O. Box 60–490, Titirangi, Auckland 0642, New Zealand
www.ekbooks.org

A CiP record for this book is available from the National Library of Australia.

ISBN 978-1-925335-24-8

Designed by Big Cat Design
Typeset in Warnock Pro 20/33pt
Printed in China

This book uses paper sourced under ISO 14001 guidelines from well-managed forests and other controlled sources.

10 9 8 7 6 5 4 3 2 1

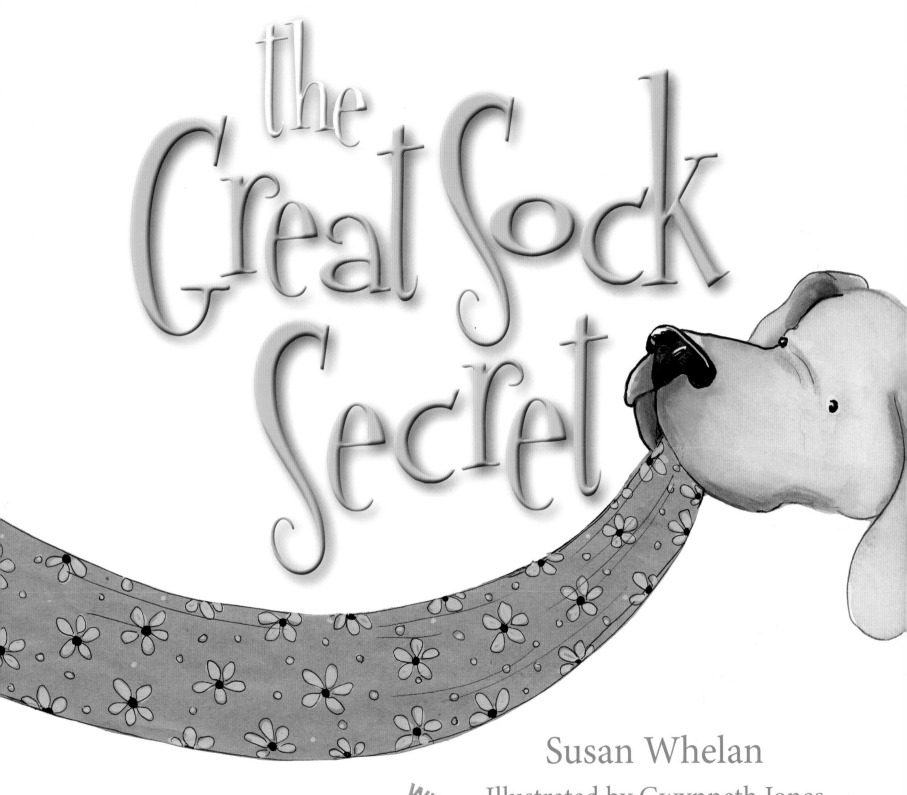

the Great Sock Secret

Susan Whelan

Illustrated by Gwynneth Jones

'I think we need to look for lost socks today,' Sarah's mother said as she looked at her basket full of odd socks.

Oh no! Sarah thought. She knew where all the odd socks were, but she didn't want her mother to find them.

'Maybe we could take Max for a walk instead,' Sarah suggested.

'Maybe we can walk Max once all the socks are found,' replied her mother. 'I think we should start in your bedroom.'

Sarah followed her mother into her room. She
quickly looked under her bed while her mother
checked the bottom of the wardrobe.

'Maybe there are some behind the door', said Sarah, trying to distract her mother.

'Nothing here,' her
mother said with a
sigh. 'Let's check the
bathroom next.'

'Still nothing!' Sarah's mother was starting to sound a little bit frustrated. 'Maybe we'll find something in the family room.'

In the family room, Sarah's mother got down on her hands and knees to check under the furniture.

Sarah checked behind her
father's favourite chair.

'We can't put it off any longer,' her mother said with a sigh. 'It's time to check your brother's room.'

'Maybe we shouldn't bother in there,' Sarah
suggested. 'You know what his room's like!'

'I think we should at least try,' her mother replied. 'Who knows what we might discover?'

That's what Sarah
was worried about.

While her mother started picking
up dirty clothes off the floor, Sarah
checked under Thomas's bed.

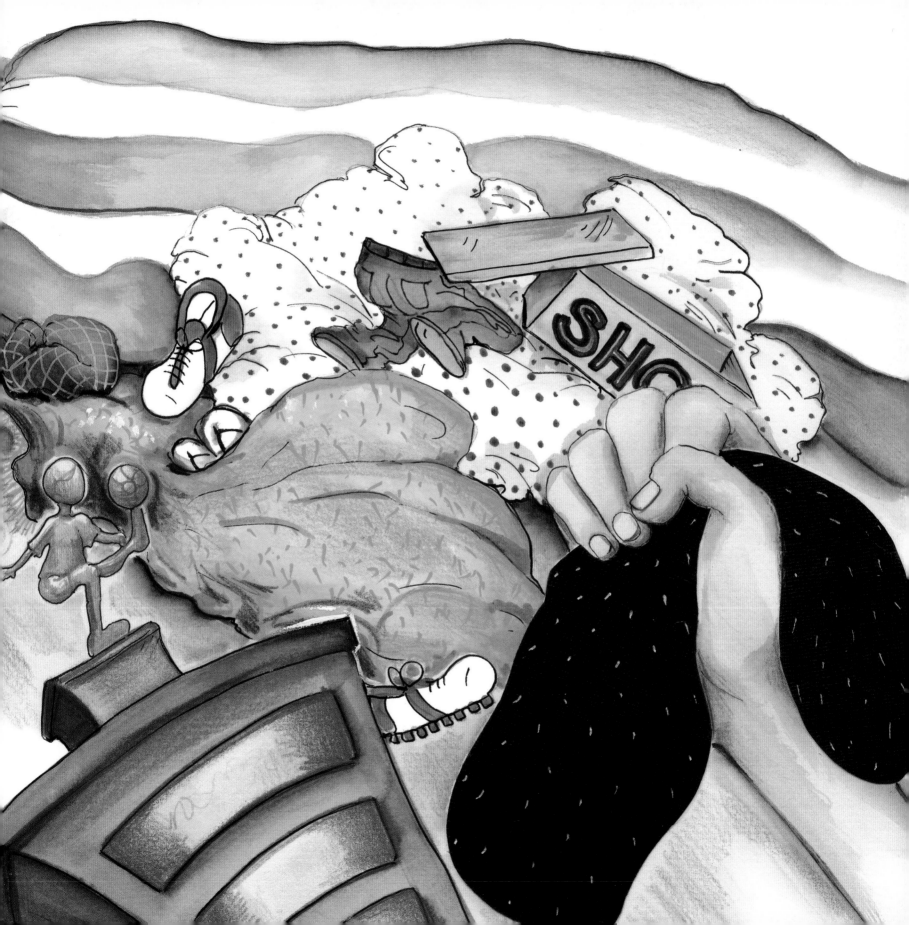

'Well', said her mother at last. 'I guess we've found two socks, so that's better than nothing.'

Sarah sighed with relief. The fairies were safe.

'Now I think we should go
hunting for lost pens.'

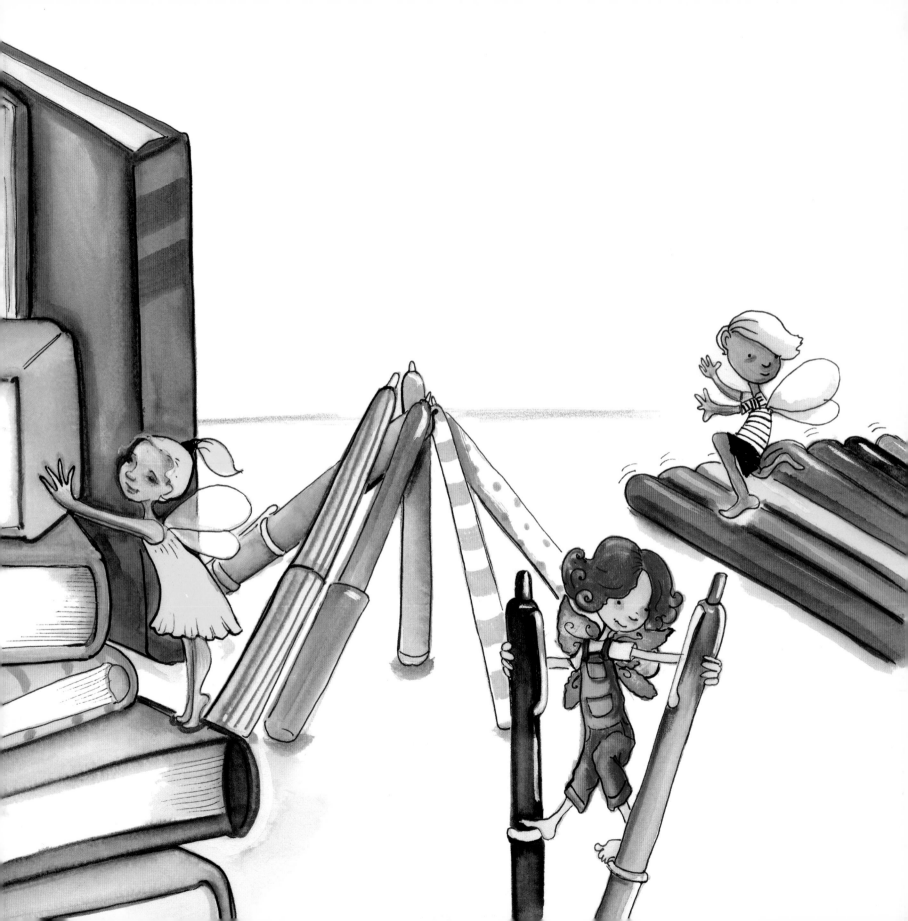